I0732350

AFTER THE GUSHING RAIN

ADAM CHRISTOPHER MOORHEAD

ISBN 978-1-959182-90-0 (paperback)
ISBN 978-1-959182-91-7 (digital)

Copyright © 2023 by Adam Christopher Moorhead

All rights reserved. No part of this publication may be reproduced, distributed, or transmitted in any form or by any means, including photocopying, recording, or other electronic or mechanical methods without the prior written permission of the publisher. For permission requests, solicit the publisher via the address below.

Rushmore Press LLC
1 800 460 9188
www.rushmorepress.com

Printed in the United States of America

But Only Words

It is without a doubt
No hesitation
That I listen to your voice
As you speak.
Words of truth seem to settle toward the top
Sounds peaceful and serene
Unlike anything I have ever heard or seen
Before.

Will these words last?
For longer than a lifetime?
Will you still remember me and I you?
Or will we simply forget each other forever
Dropped words, sinking below the ocean floor?

Simply let them be remembered
For what they are
And for how they sound
To you and not to another
Your place
Is found without a doubt
And I hope it will be there
To stay, to remain.
I have not found anything quite the same.

Landing

Going up and up
Soaring above the clouds
Man was meant to live above it all

On the ground would be too easy
Too safe
But there is where I differ

Handle a maneuver
Make way for the landing gear
Make sense only to drop lower

Now under the clouds
Closer to the end of the ride
Brace yourself and hold on

Steering and generated energy
Comes to a slow
A landing underway
And it has taken my breath away

Hear

If I never told you of your talent
If I never mentioned your name to anyone else
If I never heard you except the first time
Hear me now.

If you feel I have left you behind
If it seems I chose to industrialize
If I forgot how to say it right
Hear me now.

If you find yourself alone one day
Wondering if anyone will remember how you were
If you start to doubt love exists
Hear it now.

Stay Here

I can't move.
I want to,
But I am here.
The familiar is too important.
Do I want to be where you are?
I can visit but only to return
To where I live.
I can't move.
Where the best is: shouldn't I want to transfer?
Where I rest is: shouldn't I dwell and defer?
Every square inch of safety on the planet
Is only for the lucky
And I believe I am.
Does it matter where I stand
In the morning hours?
I can't move.
I have enough space right here.
Only enough to gather what may be missing:
Where you are.
But I have enough.
Allow me to visit but
Ask me to move no more
Out of this airless space
Until I can remain simple no more.

Journeyman's Prayer

Lord, grant me the strength I need to finish the day
Hear my cries from every tear you wash away
Lord, watch over my friends as you see them relief
Gather your followers as they stumble and believe
Lord, help me to ponder your way of life
And lead me when the day turns into night
Lord, grant me the desires of my heart
Be every day yet another new start
Lord, give me health as you see fit
May I be ready when I slow to exist
Lord, may you be honored by my life
And in the end, lead me to your eternal light

Raging Ocean

Quiet water rests in peace.
I stand firm
On the sand and dust and pieces of shell.
When winds stir up the surf
And wash away the beach with the currents of the earth,
The ocean rages, and I seek shelter and cover.
Down pours the rain and the sky darkens.
Lightning grumbles in the distance and gets closer with flashes of
electric.
The ocean rages and rages, daring me to leave the shelter.
Even with a float I would not go,
I know better.
The ocean claims more than being capable
Of demanding my attention.
The ocean expects nothing and gives nothing in return.
The ocean could care less.
Maybe I give it too much attention.
Regardless, the waves rage on and on.
And I finally recline under cover in a pocket of peace.
Safe at last, from nature's escapade.
I am not washed away this day.
I keep the lights off, watching
And watching, and watching
Until the rain stops pounding
And it may be safe to move forward.

Dance

System moving beat becoming
Pounding rhythm moving and sweating
Knocked me off my seat at the bar
Toward the front where the lights are
You see and you wait and you notice
I take my drink as the music is in front of us
I stop and spin to the beat becoming us
Slowly attract our bodies get closer
Until I drop my drink near the poster
Of Michael Jackson breaking it down, and I am closer
To where I remember my lack of step wise;
I smile at the poster and acknowledge I won't be closer
To learning to dance at least not this night
I am so much in a daze that I might not step right
So, I return to the bar and order yet another
Others join me as the hour gets later
One night I will learn the step or the dance
Until then I will stare at this poster in only a trance

Vegas or Nothing at All

Take me away but not in this state
Take me away and let's forget yesterday
Take me south-west where the air is dry and clean
Take me where waters flow as river and stream
Vegas, where your friends are
Vegas, where you can see the stars
Vegas, where the nights go on and on
Vegas, where the lights are always on
The fountains are ready there is no delay
Hop on an airplane and be ready to stay
Go with a friend or two you won't regret it
You may make a friend or two you'll never forget it
Watch your spending and always have fun
Who knows, you may only come back if you are up and have won

Gravity

A long pull that lasts longer than a lifetime
A drawing in to the center of the planet
A force greater than a person can go up against
A reckoning to handle or to try to manage

A natural existence in close proximity -
To a mass large enough to hold every human to infinity

Inevitable law of attraction
Yet it always exists
A pulling and pulling toward the ground
Gravity helps the human take a first step

Both on earth and on the moon
One day gravity may help a human walk on Mars too
And then the next planet over
Until the universe is explored and covered

Gravity will always exist
And it will stay true and real
Rain will always fall
With gravity's permission, we humans can feel

Mercy for a Neighbor

Hello, you are my neighbor:
My confidant, my friend,
Standing outside at day's end
To all my labor.
You keep a different pace,
A different schedule to your days.
I see you when I least expect it:
When we rush in and out or
Only in passing,
My mood never clarifies my hope for our peace-making.
If I grumble it throws you off,
If I stop to chat, I hold you up and slow you down.
If I make a statement about the world, you may not agree,
You may see things totally differently
But I still enjoy your company.
So, behold, I ask you this day
Go easy on a neighbor who does not always so well relate
To you and where you are,
Your origin or age,
But I know you have traveled far
And come home for the night.
Have mercy and withhold your judgement
Until we can slow down and understand.
We could start with the weather or
Even a comment about our common shelter.
Have mercy and withhold judgement as you are able
One day I may have the courage to invite you to my table.

Connect: Person to Person

Dig deep, take me under
Below the surface
Get passed the small talk.
Pretend me not,
I know there is nothing holding you back;
Don't restrain the ocean tides
If you need to cry: cry.
If you need to yell, just don't walk out,
Do tell;
I won't hold you to anything you say
I won't be afraid to get closer to you
We are only two.
I don't need to use what you say;
I will listen completely without judgement or personal decay
I will set my trust in you
And if you dropped off and were fallen behind
By another for another,
That's where we can pick up.
Lift up your chin and speak out
Take me seriously and without a doubt
I will mention only one more thing: I can't turn back the hands of time
Or change anything of how you feel about the past
But I will do my best to connect
And stay present, make this last;
As long as you have the courage to trust again,
We can connect in the end.

The World Is Bigger Than Here

If you don't say hello
If you choose to ignore
If you are always too busy or too hip or too classy
If you are always on the move
Your world is alive
But the world is bigger than here

If I describe
Everything I see
There will always be one who lives differently
Somewhere in the corner of a neighborhood
Undercover
Maybe just down the street or the next country over
Some days the world is enough
Other days my world is too narrow or too tough
Still, the world is bigger than here

It makes me happy
That I am not at the center
Of a world filled with diversity and pleasure.
What to make of sadness and tragedy?
I will seek to do my part
To make love and peace
In the place nearest to us.
It may be as simple as taking the bus.
I won't argue, the world is bigger than here.

True Peacemaker

Surrender
Lay down your weapons
Place yourself least among your friends

Avoid
A quarrel heated and ongoing
Seeking shelter from the thunderous rage

Remember
No perfect place
Is the earth, with humans reflecting a divine face

A first image made once created
A second made to compliment not to counter
An offspring of whom lived perfect

Until one day others had enough
Of him
Saying he was God's son

But this one had not had enough
He beat death on a cross
Only to appear alive as others had thought

In the image of a peacemaker
I seek and find
Though I make errors, I quest to be of his kind

Sea Foam

After it rains, the ocean surf seems to calm.
If the wind dies down, and the sun slowly descends,
There will still be white suds gracing the sand.

The suds are from the churning and collapsing
Of such tidal forces of nature
Sea foam remains close to the beginnings of the water

It is the foam that comforts a lone beach walker
From blistering shells stuck under the path astray
The foam provides a lighter path of washing the feet along the way

The bubbles at dusk add beauty to the scene
Of water and sand and changing patterns between.
With shoes removed, I begin to feel clean.

But I stay ashore and not wade too far in
The storm might return and I might need to go back in
To the shelter from the hurricane wind.

Warmed Hot Spring

Tropical rain pours and pours.
But it's okay, no lightning to endure.
Inland we are, near a hole in the ground
Where locals say that hot water may be found.

Racing we run through the fields of mud,
Only to reach a path near a river with a flood.
Rain drops pound and pound and the trail is not easily found,
Finding the pool reveals nothing but a steaming hole in the ground

We view the remains of what looks like a stogie
Or maybe something worse, who knew, but it threw me.
Smelled terrible like some kind of substance
Somebody saw us coming and bailed at the last second.

At least they made some room for us travelers in the hot spring.
Costa Rica yields great coffee or so it would seem.
Our time ended and we had to bail
So grateful for a few minutes of heat off the beaten trail.

Turn Me into a Giver

My time is burning up,
Time alone, and time for building.
Why am I even here?
Once trained to follow a traditional path
Ending up throwing in the towel.
I was building a name, my way, my change.
I was working for only the pay,
And enduring.
So, I stopped.
I took a few months or even years' time-out.
I took a long break before I had dug myself even deeper into the pit
    of the meaningless.
My family stopped communicating, and I wondered if things would
    get worse.
I wondered what made them all so angry.
After the gushing rain fell one evening on the weekend streets,
I realized I needed to give rather than take.
Maybe not give to the whole world, but maybe to those who would
    be able to receive.
Maybe my family would receive, or maybe I would drift from them
    and fast.
But there was no other way
For me to go on
Than hope to give and to forgive.
I could not run any more, I could not hurry through each day.
I'm sorry but I tried, I tried.
Forced to refocus on those that would need a shoulder to cry on or a
    tear to finally fall.

Yes, sister.
Yes brother, I am here.
But maybe all I can do is pray for rain,
And hope for peace when the storm settles.

Wild Respect

Will you believe in me?
Will you cast down your doubt for a moment?
Will you set aside a critical ear for a day and a night?
Suspend our quarrel and teasing only for a blink second?

You won't understand it, but I believe in you.
I believe in us.
It's why I do what I do.

You do what you must.
But I believe in us.

Get a Grip

(Inspired by the sound of "Lazybones" by Soul Coughing)

Today, yet another
Way to forget what I am supposed to be working on.
Strangled with boredom, yet maintaining long anticipation
With hope.
I feel uneasy.
With worries about the future and prosperity
Worries about so many distractions and lack of drive.
But I am not like the majority.
Listening to a tune from the university days
Brings back old feelings of being young and a little fearless,
Knowing that my whole life was ahead of me.
But now, now that I have aged, I am subdued.
And I know I can't return to youth.
My time is all I have, "live your dream" they say.
What if I feel like doing absolutely nothing at all today?
All I wish is to just be.
To just be.
And to be loved by at least one.
Despite all disconnection, there is only hope for one relation
With a friend for a little while, one who may help me get a grip for once
And postpone my lazy bones.

Where Do I Stand?

I caught the news today
So much data floating around
Hard to determine exactly what to say
In response

If I ever believed in anything,
It was in truth itself
So hard to see the truth these days
Among the details, and the chatter

So, I drop my pen,
Close my notebook,
And I pray for clarity to decide
Where should I stand on this topic?

I believe in mercy
I believe people make mistakes
As do I
When will the debate cease and there be no more fight?

Running Toward the Light

Dream bigger, move slower
Aging brings me to clarity
Create a world on your own,
Or accept one told from ancient days far gone
I choose to run toward the light

My time is limited
As is yours
I am not here to preach like the many who do
I am here to walk through open doors
My goal is to run toward the light

Your life is your own
And my life belongs to no one else
By faith we see the way ahead
Through love our paths may converge
And I will hope you too run toward the light

A light in the darkness
A way without fear
A hope beyond sorrow year after year
A goal to our labor
A peace in the end
To rest without struggling again

Patient

Wondrous
The day is dark
Sleepless last night
Hearing the news
From the radio
Drags me under and beneath the blues
How to make it through a day such a struggle and so heated?
I pace, slow down, listen, get away from the noise
I find a quiet place and remain seated.
I take a deep breath,
Converse with a neighbor
I ask great questions while listening to a stranger.
A friend of a friend
Once asked me if I could be happy here,
I mentioned I was not sure
In years like this year.
I break my silence and smile for a minute or two
I don't know where the smile came from
It just appeared from somewhere inside I once knew.
So, I drove back home
And only came to a wonder:
Is happiness dependent upon my interactions with others?
I finally got to the end of my day
Patience was required and the narrow pathway.
I will always remember how to recover
From days that see such dark disaster
Patience inspired, a smile can smooth over,
Wondrous break through at the end like no other.

Florida

Warm, bright days
Sometimes a gray colored sky among the water, sand and sun
Relaxing, taking a break for fun

Engaging and resting and doing it again tomorrow
These are the days along the coasts
Inland is a far different matter

Southern voices and country folks like to chatter
Rural and agriculture with occasional industrial sites
Florida spreads its gates open wide

Here is where I began my days, where I was born
Will it one day be the place where I am taken from
After all my labors are done?

And as my hat is hung on the wall,
Will Florida still be there for me when I fall?
Will there be a place for me to rest in my final days?

With everyone else from the north country
We keep filling up and filling space
I am sure everyone will help each other find their place

I'll Be a Guide

Somewhere underneath it all is a melody
A sound that is not afraid to be heard
No, not afraid to make a mistake
Not afraid to be felt for who it really is
I will be the guide;
Performance is overrated
We have all heard that line before
From almost everyone
You just don't get me, man;
Don't worry man, I'll be the guide
Maybe these words are really meant to come out
For you to fully understand;
Or maybe they are there for a broader group
For a bigger group, besides you
Don't worry I can take some advice
Polish me up, stand me up, help me speak out
For a while as I know this won't last forever even if we want it;
It's only music if people like it
It's only a song if people hear it
We have fun, we laugh and dance, and don't take me too seriously, man
After all it's only a song, man
Don't worry, I'll be the one to sing it
Have mercy, I'll be the one to cry it out
If I need to because some days I do
Just know I'll be there for you
And I'll be the guide;
So scared of making a mistake
So scared of underperforming
When what you need is no warning
I'll be that guide;

Take the expressive, with it respect
Running down the clocks of a lifetime
And I'll be the guide.

Too Many Chiefs

Dig deeper I hear
Tell them what they want to hear
Run faster, work harder
Your voice will outlast yet another;
But I have heard it all before
Heard it since the day I was born
It is one thing to create and work
It is another to finish and complete and not ignore;
Put it all out there, leave it all on the floor
They all say something different but
I always let them tell me more;
Just stop, listen, rather than go.
Just stop, attention, to where you want to go.
They say if you are determined and work hard enough
You can accomplish anything;
I guess it's a line from a movie
But I won't bring in complaining.
Let the crazy be crazy,
Give yield to the loudest ones,
Plot my steps a little more carefully
And live like tomorrow might be my last.
I will remain with the Indians.

Give My All to Love

A time I have on the earth
A time to give or to take
I must confess I tend to do both
Oh, the amends I try to make.
If all I can do is give my love to one
Is that enough?
Who else should I follow up with?
If all I can do is love you
Is that enough?
I steadily and calmly come to the end of my pursuit.
I raise the question as to the object of my love
I beg a different assumption: that I can give everything to love.
To try to throw my arms around the world would surely fail,
It is when I look skyward and see a Maker's beauty unveiled.
For everything I can see I cannot know,
But love is why I am here, come closer let me show.
To give and give my time for love,
To love far and near, below and above:
I am limited and can only do so much,
I ask for guidance, my next step toward love.
For there is where I believe and where I draw strength,
To carry on in wisdom.
One day, I will be gone,
And whether I am remembered or not,
With my body resting below a grave-marked cross
I won't be able to hear the report on how well I have done
In loving experience, in loving everyone.
I fear I am falling short as these words are donned
Have mercy, and let peace reign, if possible, when I am gone.
Help me to believe, know that I give my all to love, in attitude, in action

And in every way I know how,
It still won't be enough; Lord knows without a doubt.
I am only one man, a squirrel trying to survive
I hope one day I will be free enough to thrive
Only in love and not in fear or slavery,
If I give my all to love it will require bravery.
Peace and justice: I ask you to come
With a soulful song for not just anyone.
It is an honor to love you.

Superior

You terrify my thoughts
You boss me around
You treat me like nothing I have ever found
You hang up on me
You make fun of my chin
You have never let me in
To what you really feel

I have never seen you
Only heard your voice
You live at a pace I can barely enjoy
The Eve side comes out
Every now and then
Destructive
Mistrusted
I can't really explain why
Other than you really don't like what you hear

But when I forgive myself
And when I extend my reach for yet another night
There is where I find your influence great yet out of sight
You never seem to agree with anything I say
Or you don't understand
Or you don't really care

I feel like I have to walk on eggshells when I speak
Or you will go away
You have so many people in your life
Why do you keep looking me up?
From your world to mine
Across the telephone line
Over time, truth comes out and it's clear

Dearest Ones

Noise drives me crazy.
Like: get me out of the hurry and the city
Immediately,
Before I am cooked and grilled and can't focus or hear anymore.
If we haven't spoken in a few decades,
I guess we are forgotten.
What would you say to me anyway?
I distanced from what may be most important to you.
But forgive me if I might say: I miss you, all of you.
I miss your laughter at me, your raised eyebrows;
I miss you not quite understanding me, but trying.
I miss seeing you, and I miss your questions.
Isn't it interesting who we choose to keep up with?
And who we choose to let out of our worlds?
If I may tell you one thing it would be this:
I am sorry I could not love you better, the way you needed.
I believe I am made for certain types and have found solace with only
    a few.

Burn

Sustain me somehow, the way you know.
Use a chemical reaction if it would help us, ignite us.
I often feel cold and slumped, like coals, like remains,
Lacking expression and resting only spent and used up.
When you call my name, I perk up and listen.
I am so tired of being called every other name in the book.
Only when you call, do I grow up.
You reach for me like I am able to support you,
And you expect me to.
After all that is where I am now: grown up.
And although youth holds many fond memories,
And new experiences that I shall never forget,
I burn with anticipation and hope for the future
And the thrills that might still remain.
Sometimes it feels like God wants me to be poor,
Or I just don't have the luck to be content with what I have.
But if I am still, and listen to how I am made, I feel a heat sustained,
Sparked so long ago without a duration or a clock.
That connection to the world that only love can fill:
I am made for ecstasy.

Voice

They say we all want something beautiful…
You ask me why I stay here, far away from you
When your voice is all I hear.
Over the telephone,
It's enough for me to stay here
Your voice is sweet and filled with allure
But I can't leave for just anything I hear.
If you were closer, it may work better
Over the years your voice is all I hear,
And I have never seen you
Up close, with all the body language
And expressions I hear you make
But never see.
It's better for you to stay clear out west
It's better for you, can't you see?
After all, it may be different in person
You know you mean the world to me
But I can't make the move
All for you
Surprise me some day
Let me in on more than your voice
I love you

Go

Go
I'm sorry
Don't make another sound
Leave me here alone
And I will be alright

Go
I'm sorry
Don't let me drown
Leave me here alone
And I will still see the light

I can only love you where you are
I can only give and give so far
I can only love more and more
Until you go

I will listen to you
I can hold on to you
Just take me with you
And I will see the light
I have never felt better you know
I have all these letters you know
But I have never felt better, so go.

Vanished

Put me back together
Steady as she goes
Write it out with a feather
The light in your eyes
Shines the way home

Clearer now, I can hear it
I promise
I love it, can't you see?
I'm holding on,
I'm holding on
In the middle of the night
I can hear it
I see your love.

There is a way for you
There is a way to go
I might not be able to tell you
But I see the look in your eyes
Like it's the whole world or nothing
Or maybe it's just you are in love

Grow Up

Put it down
Let me figure this out
For once
Let me do it

Surround
But don't piss me off
I have no idea who you are
But let me do it

Grow up
Grow up
Grow up one day
Grow up
Grow up
Grow up some day

Letting Go

I had everything planned out
Now what?
On the fly, it's only failure when you try and try

To force it, to make it happen
I've only done this once,
Once.

And I thought I had let go
But too often I hold on too tight
Makes me nervous, man.

Just being honest
Trying to be real, man.

So, let's talk about what?
Let the show go on,
And not talk so much?

Let action do the sounding
And have another shot at it
Make a run of it, a go at it,
Just tell me you haven't given up yet
Listen to your true self.
It's okay
You found a way
You paved a path
To love
The only thing I could use more of

Fun runs out too much
And I am left only
With what I must give away

Hang around more
It's okay to go slow
It's okay to look
Like you want to look
And feel better

I once came around
After too many years passed
And it was you I found
Or maybe you just welcomed me back

And no, I hadn't changed too much
Only got a little older
Just got a little bit older

Crowding into Me

Tell me a little something
Let me in on a secret
One that I could give away
Give away
Stand at attention
Lead me in direction
I've only words to know

You are crowding my space
Lean into someone else
Get out of my face
For once
And tell me another secret, baby

Eternity

I once thought it was
A test
A race to success
Maybe I needed it
Until I let it go
I let it go
And decided to give away more of what I had
I remembered the ones we once heard
Nobody ever knew of them
But we did
Now, nobody cares but us
And it's not a bad thing for love
To be seen from the inside
And heard from a new side
They changed their ways
Of delivery
But you can't hold back
Eternity
Set within the vision of a
Soul
Eternity
Set within the vision of a
Soul

Outside

Sit outside
Under a night sky
Catch all the lights
And wonder
Don't laugh, you aren't in a classroom
No, not even near
But you might hear a sound
Like a heartbeat
For once
Shifting to get comfortable
Next to that special someone
If you are lucky, you may
Be given a word of light
But no need to jot it down
Or run the numbers.
Listen to the sound
Nature has a voice for you
I am not the teacher
I just listen too
And I won't tell you what to do
But it helps many days
It just does
Honest.

Stay for Vegas

What I want to say to you
I can
What I want to give to you
I will
What was meant for wealth
I found luxury
What was meant to impress
I found your eyes on me.
I came to you wanting to receive
I came to you wanting to take something back home
And you gave me more than I asked for
So much I couldn't help but give it away.
Could I stay for Vegas?
Could I stay with you a little longer?
We could make it outrageous
With what we have to give away.
Stay for Vegas
I want to stay for Vegas.

The Time Is Now

It's so warm here in the south
Even in December we never freeze
So, I looked you up
As the days drew closer to Christmas
And I guess you never thought it would be me

Many days feel so random
Luck, chance, and just preach to me
About salvation and ransom
But that's when we go outside
And say hello to our neighbor
The one right next to our door

A lot of days in the south
The neighbors don't say hello
I don't really mind . . . tight quarters, ya know?
But at least to be able to stay warm
In the winter is enough
It's what I had to let go of: control.
Or maybe my misunderstanding
Of what is meant in the south
I want to stay warm like this forever.

Where Are You Going?

Don't you remember?
Don't you recall thinking to yourself
One day you were going to leave it all
For Montana?
Do you remember?

Do you remember thinking: to hell with all of this?
Wasting time in a hurry going nowhere fast
But you did have fun too, right?
After all, you need others who care about you.

It's not in the city
Where you hear yourself think.
It's not in the hurry
Where you can actually breathe.

So, who will make noise with me?
And will they take care of us?
Many people in the outskirts are crying, you know?

So, who will make sense for us?
I will settle down to the warmth
Find a guitar and sing a melody for us.
I admit, I get scared too, you know, I admit it.

For the Soul

So, you are not the president
Of the filthy rich?
We need leaders too you know.
So, you aren't the doctor who cures the sick?
We need health don't you know.
You say you want to sing?
It's not a competition, man.
For money or for anything.
Just let us hear your tune
Like a new bird in the garden
Or the songs from sunlight upon a new day
Let it go, man. Get over yourself.
Say yes and have fun for once.
Let it come out.
I'll be there to catch you if you fall
I'll be there when you feel like you can't get up
I'll be there when you've lost it all
All for the sake of love, man.

You don't have to lose control
To give in to your desire for more.
You don't have to play rock and roll
For us to hear the songs of your soul.

Live for Now

Put out your hand
Feel the rain drops
Drink in the sunlight
Stare at the ocean longer
Climb the snowy peaks
Ride the pine needles down
Leaving nothing but love
And speak from the center of joy within.

Open up your heart to
A new beginning
Open up my love to
All things newly starting
Above your fears of growing old
And never doubting your place
Among the streets of gold

Go with me one day
Believe in a second start
Put on your top hat and gloves
We are cold now but warm is who we are.

I Saw You Today

I saw you today.
You were sitting down and speaking honestly
Words of sincerity
Serious
Among my hurry through the day
I could not get you out of my mind.

You are only an acquaintance
I don't even know your age now
You must be older than me.
And yes, you are lovely.

If it takes an ocean or a sunset to stir a heart
You are both.
If it means someone finally understands
And if it is only a crush, it's ok to flirt.

I drink in the sunlight of today
Special is our time while we have it
My friend, I will not forget you.
Look me up and let's have a rendezvous.

Giving a Voice to Love

I hear you and I want to sing out too
But I just don't know the words
All I squeak out is a hum
Until I listen about a thousand times and slowly learn
What love sounds like
What harmony might move these people, these beautiful ones.

I press the replay button over and over
Just to get another glimpse, another chance
To sing with it right this time
I listen and sing, listen and sing
It is not my song but yours I want to learn

I sing, I wonder
I listen, and ponder
I sing, then I consider
I relate, I feel the same way about what you sing
And even how you sing it.
I wonder what you were feeling too
If I sing it right, I might feel better, relate to you.

Visualize

What happens
When you can't hear live music anymore
For fear of someone shooting bullets into the audience?
What happens
When people are so scared of not having money from their labors
That they can't ever enjoy vacation?
What happens
When people get so sad and they have no solution for their mood
And no one hears or helps them?
What happened
To "lay down your weapons and arms"
In a stand for peace and truth?
You win.
Art. Poetry. Music. Love.
I will live to tell the tale
Of fantasy gone well
Of hope seen
Of dreams come true
And of old friends making new ones.
I will never sell
That which does not endure.
No product, no line would ever come close
To the real you, not what you feel enslaved to.

The Haunting

A tattoo often pushes me back
I just want to plead: tell me the story behind it.
Articulate what you won't.
But with me, it is a haunting that circles back around every now and
    then.
A prodding, a temptation, a gnawing for another better place in life.
A new dwelling in the mountains perhaps,
Or one near a waterfall or flowing river,
Or a place on the other side of the globe.
Any of the above would do fine right now.
But to move again feels so complex.
Plus, how would I survive?
I would explore,
And live free of a schedule
Of where I had to be every day,
And free of what I would have to do.
To write.
When I first started out, I hesitated
About spreading the word,
You know: letting people read
What I wrote for the world.
Call me sensitive, but I did not want to hear
I was an idiot.
But the words are there, they circle back around every day,
Calling me westward, upward, homeward.
Call it a pulling of the soul, an attraction into the future,
A plead to leave everything in the past behind,
And to fix my eyes on the rest of my life.

Belief

Tell me your story
I will listen, I have the time.
I don't have anywhere to go, right here is fine.
I will not guess, you may be upset,
From how little attention I have given
Feel free to look past our irritation, our subtle difference.
There was once a day when I was so completely happy,
Young and with the future unknown.
It is all I can do to keep from rehashing the past.
It is all I can do to keep from feeling I have wasted so much time.
They say to risk more as I go forward.
Risk could be its own reward if I survive it.
Wealth: I want it just like anyone.
But there is a limit to what I would do to achieve it,
A seat belt holding me back from just going for it.
When I carve out time for you, it seems to never be enough.
When I hear music filled with hope, it seems to come and go.
My feelings tend to be numb with gospel every once in a while,
But it is not a sustained joy I hold during these days of woe.
Should we happen to get together forever, I will say I have fallen in love.
But the kind of love I believe in is filled with reckless abandon.
The love I believe in goes beyond being parented, pastored, corrected
    until exhaustion.
The love I believe in fosters no competition.
In the end all I have is this belief in love.

Finding A Purpose

Earning a living was never my purpose
Becoming wiser was never mandatory
Schooled through a system, true I was privileged
Nothing extraordinary but breathing and living.
A quest for a thrill, live life to the full
Its ok to strut.
Walk before you run over the frequent and content.
I am so tired.
Do I stay tired alone, or will you help me along?
You worked hard to be where you are.
Help me to work harder.
You partied hard to be a great dancer.
Teach me how to dance before the day is over.
Some seem to be happy with ease,
Others you would think they should be happy but maybe they are
    faking their way.
Enjoy life.
Enjoy giving.
Giving is the way.

Wander

Let it be
So easy and so quiet
Yet not to the point of boredom
I lack the energy to analyze it.

I could write you a command
A mission
A warning if you don't
But I won't
I just can't

You might believe I indulge
Too much
Escape
Too much

Between a rock and a hard place
I only want to behave
And stay out of trouble's way
For alone I am bound to wander

Is it Too Late?

I can't think straight
Is it too late,
For me to start into a different track?
Like forget all of this and go another way
A different direction, but not back,
The one we wanted when we were young.
Aging and time passing begs me to take an easier route.
Help me realize
What is there for the taking
And it's not the fame.
Make and create, it's what you want.
Leave it up to God about whether it will become loved.
Create, be real, remember, look forward, have a dream, live.
Be clear when you tell me
That this is my life here.
Never will I give up,
Never too late when you do what you love.

Infinite Second Chances

Whistle a tune to me, just a sweet melody
That makes me feel alive again, take me
Away from my doubt of you
And from my poor lazy.
Fly me away where I can be real again
And let me feel your beat and melody.
You have never lost your chance
To make me smile again.
So, go out, dance in the dark
Evade the boring
Feel the rhythm,
And feel better today and tomorrow.
Understand you me
You have another opportunity.

Buzzed

Get me up and talk to me
I feel buzzed
I had a few glasses
But not too many,
Too many to see everything clearly
Through my eyes of dark green.

Tell me you feel it too
You feel buzzed
Did you have a glass or two?
But not too many
To help you feel better
For a while you have an answer

Like young love
I feel buzzed
Through a series of glasses
Of haze and dances;
I feel buzzed
Will you join me in this story?

Legacy

I like nice stuff, quality things . . .
Food that really settles and satisfies,
Hotels with their brilliance and sceneries.
Health of mind, soul and spirit.
I like nice clothes and the latest style.
There is something about working for hard earned that stands out.
Maybe it's less important what I do,
And more important that I just have enough to get through
To afford the finer things.
I won't be able to take anything with me when I am gone though.
Memories might remain of me in a few, hopefully they are positive ones.
But will I be remembered for being selfish or brutal?
Or will I be remembered at all?
I admit I don't fully understand the gift of opportunity I have been given
Here in America, opportunity for the finer things.
But is that what I should pursue: the finer things?
What about helping others, relieving pain,
Standing against oppression and suffering?
Generosity is possible where there is a need to fulfill.
"Give without expecting return," they say,
"Sow the seed of good news until your final day."
Help people see, help people believe even when they feel stuck.
For it is in the places of darkness where a little light can make all the
    difference.
I hope I can shine a little bit of light instead of becoming lost in the
    darkness.

What You Leave Behind

So, I am left here
And you are gone.
I am left with a few of your personal things,
I am left with memories to sort through.
But these do not help me during days of missing you.

I believe you are in paradise; heaven is what we believe.
You are now there and somehow waiting on me.
So, one day I will see you again, you told me so,
And if I believe then it's a guarantee.
Until then, I will do my best
To make every moment count
And live fearlessly.

I know it will not be easy
Some days with you gone,
But I will believe in others and in their comradery.
I will not go through the rest of my life alone.
Until I see you again, nothing is lost,
Here's to your victory.

Lift

I feel a weight of heavy lifting
Lifting
From the sound of your voice
I can't keep it inside
I will venture out to hear more
Play and play and gather in
Dance and dance to your sound
Of you
And only you
You are the one
Be the change you want to see
Until we meet again
You are my dream played out
You are my new reality

Wash Me Away

You speak so slowly
You slow me down
from my running around
Around and around.
You are so free
It is not me, now I see
Clearly.
You have me wrapped up in a world
not a mystery.
And when I was so alone,
when I was at my worst
You saw me and helped,
you picked me up
And helped me carry on
It was you and not just anyone

You found me again
So familiar you are
You are so smooth and sappy
Then you washed me away
In a moment I could not resist

Hold Your Own

I get you; I get your drift.
You want to hold your own.
You are on your own,
And great at it.
I guess you bought in to the myth
That you won't need anyone.
At least not me, at least not my two cents.
Or anything else for that matter.
I call it a myth because independence is overrated.
Freedom and quest for an audience is one thing,
Abandoning everyone in the process is something else.
What was it I said?
Or was I too heavy, asking too many questions?
I guess you are right,
I guess I give up competing for success
Like everyone says;
I guess I seek a different path and our ways diverge,
A different audience, a different definition of success.
My friend: go with God,
I will miss you.

Story of a Peaceful Place

I hear they are tearing down the towers
Where we used to live for a time so long ago.
Memory fades, yet youth reminds me as I grow.

Some days I feel like I am being prepared for something great
Like it is only a matter of time before it all comes gushing out
Like a ponded leaking roof or a waterfall or a water spout.

These days the sun goes down early
Leaving me in the dark so rapidly,
Must prepare for such a change nightly.

Made it up to a sleepy beach town today.
Early in the afternoon people strolled as a banjo slowly played
Especially soft since the afternoon was a Sunday.

Wandered into this Irish goods store
Full of real Celtic artists' fancy dining room displays,
Including green crosses on fine glasses and china plates.

So tranquil, so happy, and so elderly,
I wanted to stay in there forever.
A postcard read "I Survived Catholic School," and somehow, I felt
    better.

As I drove away, I got behind a mobile camper
With a "freedom" sign covering its spare tire.
Smiling, I steadily cruised over the island river;
Reflecting on this place brought a peace that seemed to last forever.

Taken Care Of

Crave it
Work for it
Pursue it
Struggle to get it
Until unhealthy:
Money.
Need it
Can't live without it
Going to compete for it
And compete, and compete.
Need to do this:
Money.
If I trust
That there will always be enough
Maybe not for luxury
At least not entirely
But if I trust
Do I really need a lot?
After all I will pass away one day
And everything will be granted to posterity.
How much do I really need?
How much is a lot?
I rest only in trust: that I will be taken care of
Forever.

You Can Go

My words will never be enough.
Wait
Don't go.
Stay.
Here.
For a time
And for a while.
If my words are all you can handle,
If my thoughts are too unique,
Too abstract
And too distinct,
Then I might stay
For a time
And for a while
And you can go.

Remembering Us

After the dust settles
And I listen to everyone
All the time
Every day,
You are all that is left.
So many years ago
So many memories ago
You see I always come back to you.
You have known me longer
And for other reasons
Than them, than most.
We will recover.
We can recover.

Guaranteed Certainty

So enough of the down time
Enough of the binge drinking every day
Until I mostly waste away
Every single minute.
I finally came to a realization:
My time is ticking away.
The certainty of aging settled in
And I began to wonder about where I will head after I die.
And what I might leave behind besides my name
What type of legacy.
The certainty of aging has started to get to me.
Despite how difficult school was, the long days of boring classes
And flexible "on my own" time.
In school I was trained to work and work,
To build and build strong buildings tall.
I was just so relieved to know that it ended,
And I graduated,
Like my breathing will one day,
Guaranteed.
You see, you can fantasize and dream forever,
Even when you are older
It helps pass the time
Until your dream becomes a reality.
For some it may never occur.
But back in school I will never forget the series of weeks
Where I felt contentment for the first time.
Beyond a peace, more of an oath I took:
If I never lived another day
I lived a complete and full life up to that point.

Heaven

There was a moment when I took my first breath
There will be a moment when I take my last.
The time between
Is given as a gift to share with not just anyone.
So sweet a life can be
So sensitive
Yet dependent
On love
Both from others and from above.
I believe in heaven
Where I will begin with a new breath
Where I will have a home again.

I Dream of San Francisco

Honey,
Before I knew where you came from
I often wondered about the weather and how much sun
Shines through the air over northern California.
How cool the climate
And ideal for fun.
Everything from golf to the ocean to the wineries.
A few of my favorite rock bands emerged
From that part of the country.
But it is the city I dream about, the hills and the tourists
And the food.
The buildings and the cabbies,
I dream of San Francisco,
A little north from Mexico
And on the other coast from where I rest my head.
I finally met up with you.
Even so briefly, and even so recklessly.
I am so glad I took a walk through the Wharf.
One day I will see you again.

Get Out of Anger

On this beautiful afternoon
I am still remembering you
From several days before
We spoke, or you did most of the speaking.
Where did your anger come from?
Where did you get such hatred?
I did not even know you.
I am sure it was not anger only at me, or was it?
Did you need a target?
What happened?
You kept asking me questions, refusing any answer I would give.
I told you I believed in love, and God, and peace.
You wanted no part of it.
I kept thinking it was something I said, or did, or did not say.
It is your life, but shake away your anger. Too much of it in the air
    these days.
Too much argue, too much quarrel, too much disgust and intolerance.
Coexist. Put it down, man. Lay down your weapon.
We never even really began to converse, you seemed you were on a
    mission.
This was no game, no winner, no fun, was it?
Is it fun to remain angry? I have been there, and it goes nowhere.
Much anger in my past.
But not anymore. Not today.
Our talk was not even about money. It was about love, and happiness.
Cease your anger, at least toward me,
Or tell me to be honest and what to do to fix this, to fix us.

The Value of Time

It is your life, your time, no one else's.
Your priorities are not exactly like mine.
I hear you.
But if all you want to do is correct me
You are imposing your time over mine.
If you are only going to direct me and steer me where you believe I
    should go,
Maybe we disconnect.
This is sad.
Whatever happened to becoming all things to all people.
Is it really a matter of popular, political?
Who are you, really?
And who am I, really, and for how long?
Is it really ok to be happy with your time?
Your time is just as valuable.

To Matter to More Than One

These hours are for you.
I am not busy today, not going away, not right now.
I have slowed down to drink in the beauty of the sun and the cool
    wind.
Last night was a disaster in the weather.
You do not need to fear me getting up and walking away
To somewhere or someone else.
Better yet, you have my attention, you have my ear, you have my
    focus.
Connect.
This time is not about deadlines, meetings, conferences, and schedules.
This time is not about hurry and finishing and outcomes.
This is not about entertainment or insult.
This time is about breathing.
Resting.
Enjoying the day for once.
Many options the culture offers
And I am quick to rush off toward the latest work of art or music
    show.
Yet this day I will not.
I will listen, and I will respond as an individual.
We have nothing to argue about any longer,
And you matter to more than one.

You Sound Like an Artist

When I hear your new record
All rhythm, all artist
It makes me free.
To be so noticed, so loud, and known
Must be a rush at times.
I caught your release party video
Sponsors and all
Made me wish I could have gone too,
Seen the venue,
Heard what people were saying.
But then there are the critics, the unenlightened.
I was once one of those.
Some of the album is a revelation, a dark side coming out.
Like what the hell, where is this coming from, this anger?
That stuff is hard for me to handle, at least at first.
I just skip it.
Maybe you are just getting it all out, what you need to say, what you
    need to make
Before you get too old, or us listeners get too weak to hear it.
People ask me what I listen to.
I told them it was you.
They were like, what?
Why not someone else greater?
I told them I saw you play live one night, the first night I ever heard
    of you.
It changed everything. I was sold.
Stay out of trouble,
For we love you, bro.

www.ingramcontent.com/pod-product-compliance
Lightning Source LLC
Chambersburg PA
CBHW021750190726

48290CB00008B/2556